COACH COWLES
DREAM BIG

a story about
MAKING YOUR DREAMS COME TRUE

PLAYGROUND

Every Saturday morning, Morgan woke up early, brushed her teeth, laced up her basketball shoes and headed outside to shoot hoops in her driveway.

Every night, Morgan dreamt about playing basketball for Western Kentucky University.

Ever since she was a little girl, her family had season tickets. They went to all the games to cheer for the Lady Toppers. She always told herself that one day she would be on that court playing, instead of just watching from the bleachers.

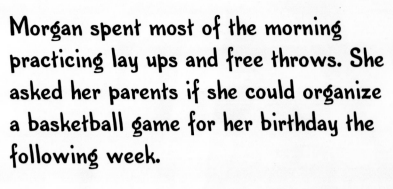

Morgan spent most of the morning practicing lay ups and free throws. She asked her parents if she could organize a basketball game for her birthday the following week.

"Sure," they replied. "It's your birthday!"

Morgan had a lot of friends, and they all played together on the school playground every day during recess. Morgan liked to play all kinds of games, but she spent most of the time on the basketball court. Her dream of becoming a Lady Topper was always in her mind.

Why do you think becoming a Lady Topper was always on Morgan's mind? **?**

The next week at school, Morgan announced to her friends that her birthday was next week. She wanted to have a big basketball game Friday after school!

6

Tommy stepped forward and said,

"Big surprise! Morgan wants to play basketball even on her birthday!"

Caleb told Tommy he was just jealous that Morgan could beat him one on one.

Morgan didn't pay much attention to Tommy. She just dribbled her basketball up and down a few times. She reminded her friends about the basketball game on Friday after school.

As recess ended, Morgan took a couple more shots and thought to herself,

"I'll show him. One day I'll be wearing that white and red uniform that says WKU across the front!"

After school Morgan went home and sat down at the kitchen table to do her homework. As she sat at the kitchen table her mom noticed that she wasn't paying attention to her work and asked her if something was wrong.

She explained that Tommy had made fun of her earlier because she wanted to play basketball at her birthday party. She didn't understand why that was so strange.

Morgan's mom walked over to her and said,

"There is no reason to feel bad for playing a basketball game at your party. You love basketball, it makes you happy, and that is the only thing that matters! I think it's great that you have found something that you love to do. Don't let anyone make you feel bad about your dreams."

Would you like to have Caleb and Tommy as your friend? Why? Why not? **?**

On Friday, Morgan woke up with a big smile on her face. It was her birthday, and more importantly it was the day of the big basketball game! Morgan wore her Lady Toppers jersey to school.

Her friend Abby was nervous because she wasn't very good at basketball. Morgan smiled and said,

"I don't mind, Abby. I just want to have fun with my friends!"

They both laughed.

The school day was finally over. All the kids headed out to the playground for the game. Morgan's parents were there with balloons and a big sign that read, "HAPPY BIRTHDAY TO OUR FUTURE LADYTOPPER!"

Morgan and her friends were excited to get the game started. Morgan's team was called WKU and the other team was called the Hilltoppers.

Tommy stood there spinning the ball on the tip of his finger. He was trying to make Morgan nervous. Morgan glared at him, but didn't say a word. Instead, she called her team together and said,

"Okay guys, let's just have a good time and play basketball!"

The game started and both teams ran up and down the court, passing to each other, making shots, missing shots and having fun. Tommy launched a beautiful jump shot. It dropped straight through the net.

"Now that's a jump shot," he turned and smiled at Morgan.

Morgan dribbled the ball back up the court and, with a beautiful cross over move, she beat Tommy to the basket. She was about to make a lay-up, when she let out a loud, "Ouch".

Tommy had fouled her and knocked her to the ground. Morgan bounced right up, dusted the gravel off her leg and headed to the free throw line for two shots.

Morgan stood at the free throw line, imagining she was in the middle of Diddle Arena. Tommy tried to mess up her concentration and chanted,

"Morgan! Morgan! Morgan!"

Swish. The first free throw was even prettier than Tommy's jump shot.

"Lucky shot," he said. "The second free throw is for the Sun Belt Conference Championship."

"Be quiet!" Leonardo shouted. "Just let her shoot her free throws!"

Morgan took a couple of dribbles, looked at the basket. She let it roll off of her fingertips towards the basket. The ball sat on the rim for what seemed an eternity, but fell to the ground. To everyone else, it was just a missed free throw. But, Morgan had let Tommy bother her and was upset with herself for missing the shot.

Why did Morgan miss the free throw? **?**

The game continued until Morgan's mom called the kids for cake and ice cream! Everyone ran over to Morgan's parents who were standing by a big cake with a picture of Big Red. Darby told Morgan to make a wish. Morgan stood in front of the cake and made a silent wish.

"One day I'm going to stand on that free throw line in a real Lady Topper uniform. I won't let anyone or anything distract me."

She blew out the candles and everyone let out a cheer! Morgan's parents said they had a surprise for her, and told everyone to shut their eyes. They counted to three and everyone opened their eyes.

COACH COWLES, the Ladytopper's Head Basketball Coach was standing right next to Morgan! Morgan was star struck. She had been watching Coach Cowles on the sidelines ever since her parents started bringing her to WKU games. She had won Sun Belt conference championships, Coach of the Year awards, and represented everything that Morgan wanted to become.

Coach Cowles put her hand on Morgan's shoulder and said, "I understand one day you're going to play for the Lady Toppers!"

Morgan told Coach Cowles that she had always dreamed of playing for WKU, but she knew that you had to be really good to make the team.

"If it's a dream of yours Morgan, then you can make it come true. I'll be there watching when it does."

Morgan's face grew red with excitement, and then Coach Cowles gave her the best birthday gift ever...Courtside tickets to the Lady Toppers game tomorrow night! Morgan was so happy, she couldn't stop smiling.

Abbey, Caleb, Darby, Leonardo and even Tommy, got an autograph and picture with Coach Cowles. Coach Cowles waved goodbye to everyone, and told Morgan that she would see her at the game the following night.

How would you feel if you met your hero? How do your feelings compare to Morgan's?

Morgan made sure her mom washed her special jersey so that she could wear it to the game. She entered Diddle Arena. The seats were packed with WKU fans cheering for their Lady Toppers. Coach Cowles invited Morgan to stand by the bench while the Lady Toppers warmed up. Mixed feelings of anxiousness and excitement came over her. She thought to herself how badly she wanted to be one of those players on the court one day.

Coach Cowles explained to Morgan that all of those players were once where she was right now.

"They all had dreams of playing at WKU and they've made that dream come true by giving a CHAMPIONSHIP EFFORT, and so can you."

Morgan glanced up at her and replied,

"I hope so, Coach."

"I KNOW so!" Coach Cowles responded confidently.

23

Morgan sat with her parents and watched the game. Darby and Caleb sat right behind her, cheering on the Lady Toppers. Morgan watched the players, studying their moves, amazed by how high they jumped, how quickly they ran, and how well they passed the ball.

"They're really good," she said to her parents. Her parents nodded their heads and told her that Coach Cowles has worked hard to make the Toppers a great team. Her dad asked Morgan if she knew that Coach Cowles was a Lady Topper before she coached at WKU. Morgan had no idea. She also didn't know that Coach Cowles was a Gatorade All-American at Marshall County High School.

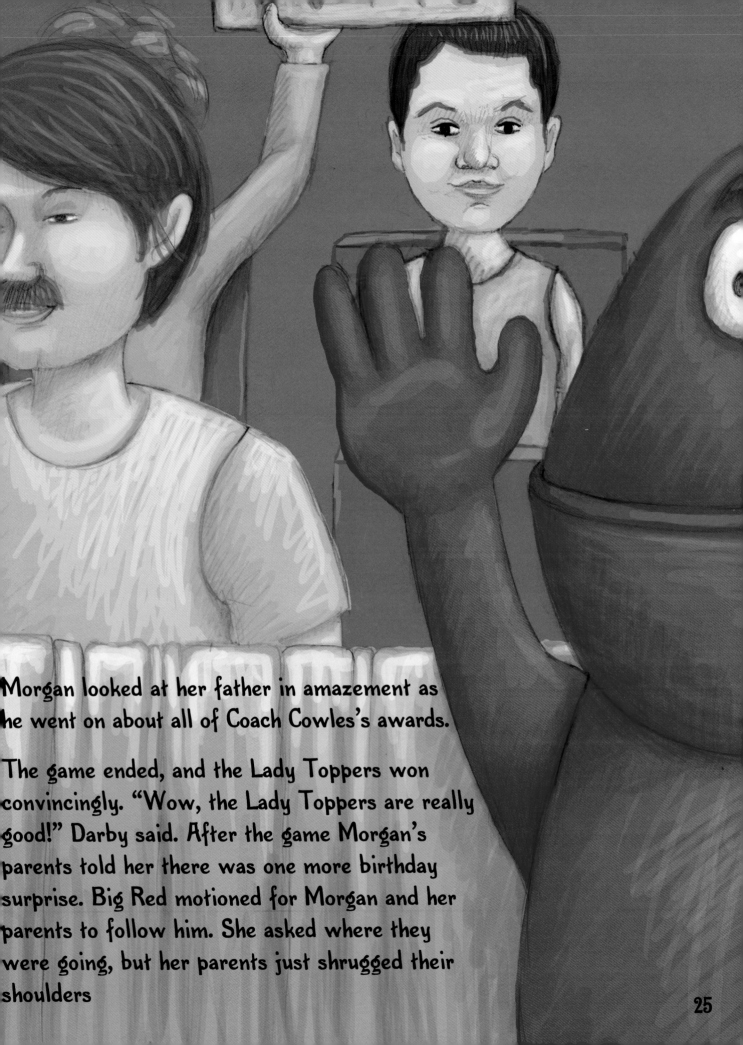

Morgan looked at her father in amazement as he went on about all of Coach Cowles's awards.

The game ended, and the Lady Toppers won convincingly. "Wow, the Lady Toppers are really good!" Darby said. After the game Morgan's parents told her there was one more birthday surprise. Big Red motioned for Morgan and her parents to follow him. She asked where they were going, but her parents just shrugged their shoulders

Big Red led Morgan into the Lady Topper's locker room. The players on the team were celebrating their victory. Big Red and Morgan walked over to Coach Cowles.

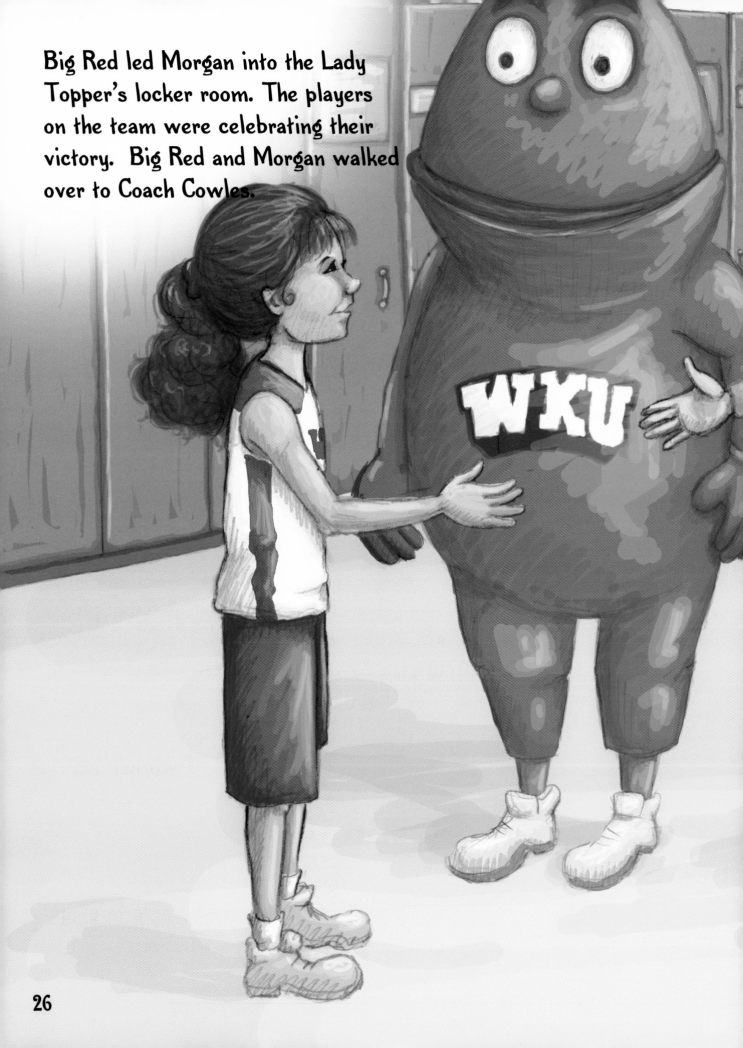

"Hey Morgan! Thanks for coming to our game, I hope you enjoyed it," Coach Cowles said.

"I sure did Coach. Thank you again for the tickets. It was the best birthday present ever!"

Coach Cowles smiled and asked Morgan if she was still working hard in school. Morgan said that she was studying hard and practicing her basketball skills everyday. She wanted so badly to be a Lady Topper one day, and Coach Cowles could tell.

"I once had that very same dream when I was a little girl, probably when I was about your age. I always knew I wanted to play AND coach at WKU. So, I worked hard and did everything I could to make that dream come true. Not everyone thought I would make it. I worked hard to prove them wrong, and to prove to myself that I could do it."

Morgan thought about how Tommy told her that she would never be able to play at WKU.

Coach Cowles told Morgan that there would be many obstacles along the way. Some people might tell her she can't or it's not possible. Coach reminded Morgan not to lose sight of her goals, and to always believe in herself and work hard! Morgan listened closely.

"One day you'll be in this locker room suiting up in one of these..." Coach Cowles tossed Morgan a real team jersey that was signed by the whole team and coaching staff.

Morgan thanked Coach Cowles and promised to not let anyone ever get in the way of her dream. Morgan really felt inspired.

Coach Cowles put her hand on Morgan's shoulder and said,

"Remember, believe in yourself, and work hard.
You can make your dream come true if you want it badly enough."

Morgan said, "Thank you Coach, I won't forget."

Morgan walked out of the locker room feeling more confident and encouraged than ever before. Her dream of playing basketball at WKU no longer seemed to be that far out of her reach. It was a dream she could achieve through hard work and believing in herself.

List three gifts Coach Cowles gave to Morgan to help her achieve her goal.

When Morgan got to school on Monday she brought the signed jersey for show and tell. When it was her turn to share, she stood up in front of the class and told them all about the game on Saturday and meeting Coach Cowles. She showed her classmates the jersey signed by the whole team and said that if she worked hard, one day she would be wearing one just like it at WKU!

The teacher, Mrs. Adams, walked to the front of the room where Morgan was standing and said, "That's a really special gift Morgan. I am confident you will achieve your goal. Who is your favorite person on the team?" Mrs. Adams asked.

Morgan held up the jersey, and without hesitation replied,

"Coach Cowles!

When I grow up,
I want to be just like her."

Follow Your Dreams... Learn To Read!

Drobocky Orthodontics believes in dreams and believes that every child has the right to follow their dreams, that's why **Drobocky Orthodontics** is a proud partner of the "Follow Your Dreams!" literacy initiative along with Western Kentucky University, Bowling Green City and Warren County Schools.

By helping provide a new and interesting platform for school literacy programs with this new book, *"Dream Big"*, **Drobocky Orthodontics** is taking a leadership role for the children of Bowling Green and Warren County with this partnership, and continuing

it's role in community support and outreach for the future success and dreams of our children.

Drobocky Orthodontics provides the highest quality orthodontic care in a loving, caring manner at an affordable cost, all in an atmosphere that is enriching to both patients and staff.

Drobocky Orthodontics continues to provide *miles-of-smiles* for their patients with their orthodontic care, but now can offer smiles for this new literacy program.

Bowling Green	Glasgow	Franklin
727 US 31-W Bypass	203 Professional Drive	927 Brookhaven Road
270.843.8556	270.651.6862	270.586.7444